TO ELLIOTT & COOPER ...

JULIA is A REAL PERSON & A
GRAND-DAUGHTER of OUR GOOD FRIENDS,
PENNY & FRITZ ...

THE AUTHOR, HEIDI, is THEIR DAUGHTER
(JULIA is HEIDI'S NEICE).

ABBEY, THE ARTIST, is ANOTHER NEICE
of HEIDI'S.

I KNOW YOU'LL ENJOY THE BOOK.

Love You, LOTS ...

MiMi & PAPA

MERRY CHRISTMAS, 2020

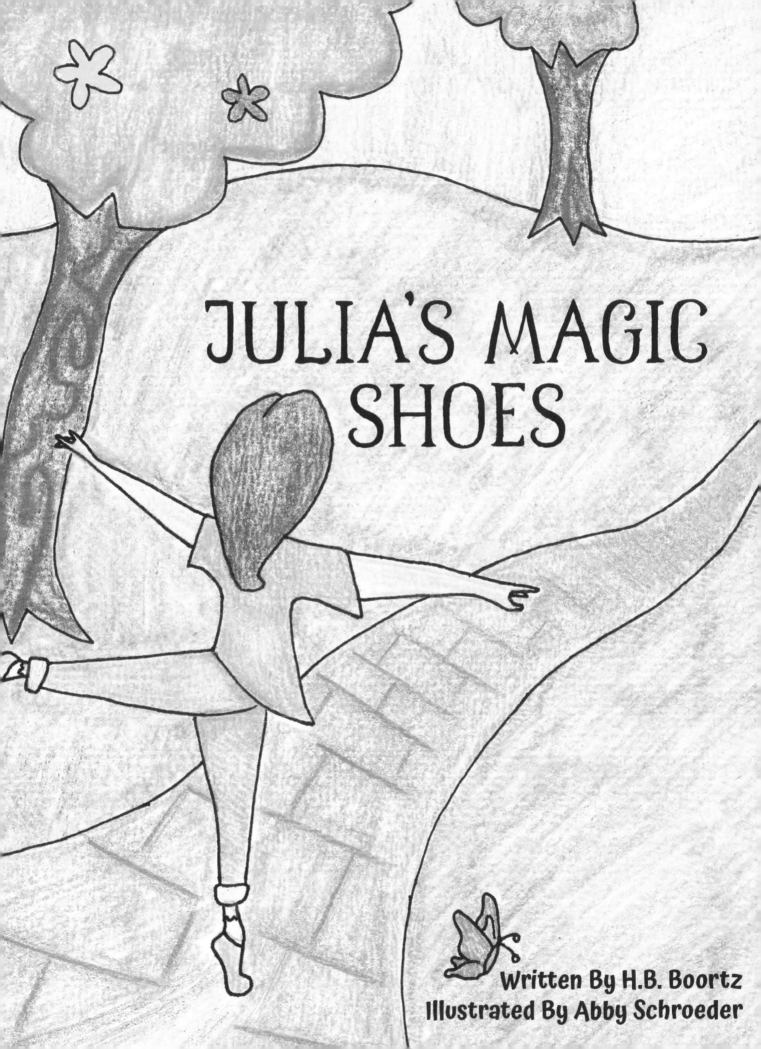

JULIA'S MAGIC SHOES

Written By H.B. Boortz
Illustrated By Abby Schroeder

Julia, you are the

inspiration for this book. You

are amazing how you color your

whole world just by dancing in it.

Much love,
Aunt Heidi

On the edge of a great, dark forest, there lived a lovely girl named Julia who wore colorful clothing. She lived in a colorful house, on a colorful street, in a colorful town. Everywhere she went, there was color.

Houses were painted in lovely hues of blues, pinks, purples, and reds. The streets were paved in oranges and yellows and greens.

Trees grew in every yard, shining with bright green leaves and flowering with all the colors of the rainbow.

*H*owever, on the edge of the colorful town,

there was a forest that was not colorful.

The forest was black and gray

and full of shadows.

The townspeople called it the

Monochrome Forest, and all the children were

forbidden to enter it.

No one knew what lived in the forest,

but it had to be evil if it made its home in such a

dark place.

The Monochrome Forest was

no place for children.

Julia never went into the forest.
She wasn't afraid of it, but she
knew she should follow the rules.
The townspeople thought the forest
was dark, evil, and angry—not happy
and safe like their colorful town.
Julia, though, thought the forest must be sad.
She knew she would be sad if she didn't have all
the color in her world.
Every day she went to school,
she passed by the forest's edge.
How she longed to paint the trees
and the grass and the streams,
for one of her favorite things to
do is to color.
Surely if there was as much color in
the forest as there was in the town,
the townspeople wouldn't be afraid anymore, and the
forest wouldn't be sad anymore.

Julia's other favorite thing in the
whole world was dancing.
Oh, how she loved to dance!

She danced around the house,
she danced her way to school,
she danced home.
Everywhere she went, she danced.
She never stopped dancing,
except when she was asleep.

One day, on her way to school,
Julia heard crying from the
Monochrome Forest.
It was a soft cry, like it came from someone sad.
Julia tip-toed closer. She heard the crying again. Closer
she went, until she was right
at the edge of the forest.
Concerned, she looked around.
She really shouldn't be this close to the
Monochrome Forest. She heard the sound again.

"Who is that?" whispered Julia.

The voice whispered back,
like wind through the trees,

"It is I, the forest."

"Why do you cry?"

"Because I'm lonely.
I see children walk by me,
but none of them come to visit me.
They don't explore my paths,
wade in my streams, climb my trees,
or smell my flowers.
Why don't the children come to play?"

Julia hung her head,
sad for the forest.
How lonely would that be, to not have friends?
How sad to live in the dark and be all alone.

"We aren't allowed to; it's forbidden."

The forest whispered back,
"I just really want a friend."

At that, the branches of the trees
seemed to droop, and the
shadows appeared darker.

"*I* can be your friend!" said Julia.

She knew she wasn't allowed in the forest,
but she thought it would be okay if she was its friend,
as long as she never went into the
Monochrome Forest.

"Really?" The forest seemed to sniff,
and the tree branches seemed to straighten
just a little.

"Of course," replied Julia.
"I'll stop by to see
you every day after school."

"That would be wonderful!"
cried the forest.

And, so, every day after school,

Julia would dance straight to the forest's edge.

She would tell the forest about her day at school

and the new picture she was coloring,

and the forest would tell her about the path

that led to the waterfall, and the warmth

of the sunrise, and the sparkle of the night sky.

One day, as Julia was twirling away from school at the end of the day, a butterfly landed right on her nose! It flapped its wings a few times, and leapt off her nose and into the air, fluttering and twirling, as if it was dancing in midair.

"*I*t wants to dance with me!"
thought Julia. And she twirled
away after it,
following from the ground the
butterfly's movements in the air. And
she forgot all about the
Monochrome Forest.

As the butterfly fluttered, Julia twirled. Together, they went down the lane and closer and closer to the Monochrome Forest. The butterfly flew straight into the forest, and Julia danced after it, not even noticing where they were.

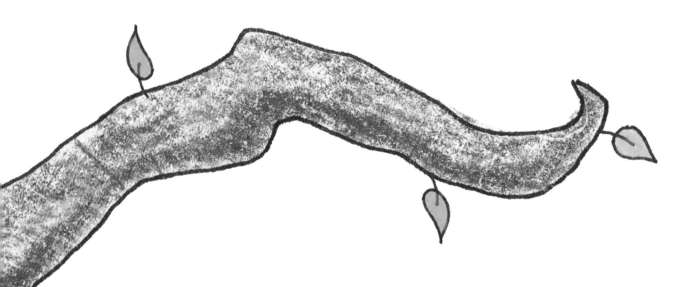

As soon as her toe touched the gray floor of the Monochrome Forest, a rainbow of color ignited from her shoes and spread to the nearby trees and the flowers. She took another step. More color surrounded her. She followed the butterfly, twirled, and the color reached the tops of the trees.

Julia just danced, and

did not notice the colors

surrounding her, where

once there was gray.

All she noticed

was the dance.

Julia heard a waterfall.
She opened her eyes and didn't
recognize her surroundings.
She stopped and stared,
and she was a little bit afraid.

"You came to see my waterfall,"
cried a familiar voice.

It was her friend the forest,
but the voice was much closer
than it was at her spot at the edge.

"I'm so glad you're here."

"Oh! Hello, forest. I'm sorry,
but I must go. Would you tell me
the way home, please?"

"Of course, my friend. Just turn
around and follow the trail."

Julia turned around and noticed,
for the first time, the dark greens of the trees,
the blue of the waterfall, the brightly
colored birds, and the carpet of
forest flowers in every color at her feet.
There, sprawled out before her, was a
path that led home.

She danced, completely unafraid
after having found herself inside the
Monochrome Forest, down the path.
When she reached the edge of the forest,
a crowd had gathered.

"I can't believe it," one person said.

"It's amazing," said another.

"It's not scary anymore," said one of
Julia's classmates.

The townspeople were staring at the
Monochrome Forest, which wasn't
monochrome anymore.
Instead, it was like a rainbow,
a choreographed dance of color that
delighted their eyes.
Their eyes fell on Julia.

"Julia, what happened?" asked her teacher.
"What do you mean?" asked Julia.

Her teacher couldn't believe her eyes.

"Well, what happened to the
Monochrome Forest?"

Julia looked back. She looked at her shoes.

"I think my shoes must be magic, because
the forest was dark and gray before I went inside, and
then I accidentally followed the butterfly
into the forest, and the next thing I knew, everywhere
my shoes touched became bright with color, just like
one of my canvases."

The forest whispered,
"It's not your shoes, my friend, it is the joy in your heart
that brought me the colors of the rainbow."

It was then that she realized that she alone could
bring color and light to the darkness of her world. It
wasn't the shoes that
were magic, it was her dancing heart.

*H*eidi Boortz grew up in Minnetonka,
Minnesota, dreaming of becoming a
children's book author.
She graduated with a degree in English and an
emphasis in creative writing from the University
of Wisconsin-Eau Claire. Shortly after, she
married an Air Force guy and has since
lived in Mississippi, Arkansas, New Mexico,
Georgia, and currently resides in Oklahoma
with her husband, two boys, and three dogs.
Although she's been writing children's stories
for her two nieces for many years, this is her
first published children's book.

Abby Schroeder is a high school student in Edmond, Oklahoma. She takes a variety of challenging courses at school, but enjoys art class the most. In addition to art classes, she does many art projects at home, from painting her own clothes to chalking the driveway. She is undecided about what to study after graduation, but is interested in engineering and architecture.